There's No Deer Around Here

Joyfully written by **Andy Hussey**
Beautifully illustrated by **Rosie Venner**

MUDDY LITTLE BOOTS PUBLISHING

It was the weekend and Jacob was staying with
Granny, but they were stuck indoors.

Earlier in the year, Granny had suggested they grow their own plants.

Jacob loved the idea. He wanted to grow a pumpkin the size of his head . . .

. . . and the biggest, brightest sunflower in the street.

Finally, the sun came out from behind the clouds.

Jacob rushed downstairs and out into
the garden to check on their plants.

He was happy to see that the sunflowers had grown,
but what had happened to the vegetable patch?
Everything had been eaten!

Granny came outside to see what was wrong.
She pointed to the gate, looking confused.

"Jacob, did you leave the gate open?
How many times have I told you to shut
the gate so Archie-Dog can't escape?!"

"Sorry, Granny!"
Jacob replied.

Jacob picked up a lettuce leaf
that had been left on the lawn.
The leaf had been nibbled.

"What do you think came
in last night?" Jacob asked.
"A cow? Some sheep?
Or maybe a deer?"

Granny was quick to reply,

"A deer?! Oh no dear, there's no deer around here!"

Every Sunday, Jacob and Granny took
Archie-Dog for a walk. Jacob would skip along
the path and splash in the muddy puddles.

Jacob and Archie-Dog were the best of friends.

Looking down in the squelchy mud
Jacob could see his footprints
and Archie-Dog's pawprints.
But there were other prints, too!

"What makes marks like this?" Jacob wondered.
"A tiny lady with pointy shoes?"

"Don't be silly," Granny replied, climbing over the stile in her old wellies. "Tiny ladies would never walk in the mud in their best pointy shoes."

"Maybe a deer?" wondered Jacob.

Granny was quick to reply,
**"A deer?! Oh no dear,
there's no deer around here!"**

When they reached the park they let Archie-Dog off the lead.
He ran round and round, chasing his ball and barking with joy.

Suddenly, Archie-Dog dropped his ball and
set off across the field, towards the fence.
No matter how loudly Jacob and Granny
shouted, he kept on running.

Finally, Granny caught up with him and put his lead back on.
But Archie-Dog kept on sniffing.

"What can he smell? A cat? A fox?
Or maybe a deer?" asked Jacob.

Granny was quick to reply,

**"A deer?! Oh no dear,
there's no deer around here!"**

The park was normally full of activity,
but today it was quiet.

Instead of the usual games and children playing,
there was only the noise of the birds, tweeting
and chattering as they swooped to catch flies.

Jacob looked up and spotted a blackbird on the fence.
The bird flapped its wings and flew away, but Jacob
noticed he'd left something behind.

Jacob reached up and carefully picked a clump of fur off the fence.

He looked at it closely. "Who could be missing this?" he wondered.

"Could it be a deer?" he asked.

Granny was quick to reply,
**"A deer?! Oh no dear,
there's no deer around here!"**

Suddenly, Archie-Dog stuck
his head into the bushes and
wouldn't come out.

"Archie, no!" shouted Granny.
It was clear he was eating
something he shouldn't.

Granny pulled him out of the bushes and Jacob expected
to see him chewing a mouldy old sandwich or an apple.
After all, they were Archie-Dog's favourites!

Jacob saw what looked like melted chocolate raisins.
Granny insisted that he mustn't try and eat one!

"Is it poo, Granny?"
Jacob asked.

"Some kind of sticky
rabbit poo? Or is it a deer?
Has it been to the loo?"
he chuckled.

Granny was quick to reply,

**"A deer?! Oh no dear,
there's no deer around here!"**

On the edge of the wood, there was
Jacob's tree. He had planted it with his
school friends, as part of a nature project.

Jacob loved seeing how much his tree had grown.
It was still taller than him, but he was catching up fast.

But the tree looked sad. The bark on one side had
been damaged and the ground had been churned up.
"What could have done this? Could it be a deer?"
Jacob asked.

Granny was weary and quick to reply,

"A deer?! Oh no dear,
there's no deer around here!"

That evening, back at the house, Jacob emptied
his pocket and studied the fur closely under
his bedside light.

He couldn't stop thinking about
the clues he'd seen that day:

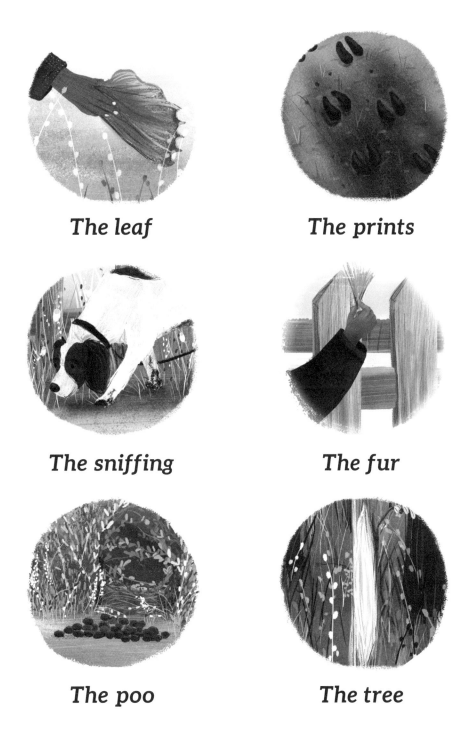

The leaf

The prints

The sniffing

The fur

The poo

The tree

Could there **really**
be deer so close to here?

Before turning off his light, Jacob jumped out of bed and
peeped out the window for one last look at the garden.
"Oh no!" he gasped. "The gate's open again!"

Before he had time to tell Granny, a pair of ears appeared
over the fence, casting a strange shadow in the moonlight.
What could it be?

"I knew it! I knew it!
A deer! A deer! So there
ARE deer around here!"

The mummy deer and her baby strolled in through the open gate and began to nibble on the few remaining leaves. Jacob smiled with delight. And, with a lettuce leaf in her mouth, Jacob could've sworn the deer smiled back.

Jacob couldn't believe his luck!
Leaving the deer to enjoy their snack,
he climbed back into bed and fell fast asleep.

We hope you've enjoyed this book and feel inspired to explore!

You may want to go on a photo treasure hunt in nature
– in your garden, street or nearest park.

Create one or two photos from the following ideas using a camera
or a smartphone (with permission of course). We'd love to see
your photos, so please ask an adult to share them on Instagram
at **@mlbbooks @lookagainphotos #naturehunt**

Take your time. Slow down, look again and see...

Before you create a photo you may want to listen to any sounds
you can hear, and touch or even smell what you've found.

1. Look closely at plants and flowers. What colours do you see?

2. Look down at the floor. What marks or textures can you see?

3. Look up at the sky. What patterns do you see?

4. Look around you, turning slowly.
What can you see that's in the light or the dark?

5. Look closely at a tree. What can you see (bark, roots, branches, leaves)?

6. What signs of wildlife and nature can you spot?

*Repeat these activities over time to see how things change with
the time of day, the weather and through the seasons. **Enjoy!***